For Frieda and Orla,
never parted for long

Henry Holt and Company, *Publishers since 1866*
Henry Holt® is a registered trademark of Macmillan Publishing Group, LLC
120 Broadway, New York, NY 10271 • mackids.com

Copyright © 2018 by Helen Stephens
All rights reserved.

Library of Congress Cataloging-in-Publication Data is available.
ISBN 978-1-250-23079-9

Our books may be purchased in bulk for promotional, educational, or
business use. Please contact your local bookseller or the Macmillan
Corporate and Premium Sales Department at (800) 221-7945 ext. 5442
or by email at MacmillanSpecialMarkets@macmillan.com.

Originally published in 2018 in the United Kingdom by Alison Green Books,
an imprint of Scholastic Children's Books

First American edition, 2019
Printed in China by RR Donnelley Asia Printing Solutions Ltd.,
Dongguan City, Guangdong Province

10 9 8 7 6 5 4 3 2 1

How to Hide a Lion at Christmas

Helen Stephens

Henry Holt and Company

New York

It was Christmas Eve, and Iris and her family were getting ready to set off for her Auntie Sarah's. Iris was very excited. "You'll love Christmas!" she said to her lion. The lion had lived with Iris ever since he arrived in town, and all the townspeople loved him.

But Mom and Dad said the lion had to stay behind.
"You can't take a lion on a train," said Mom.
"The people in Auntie Sarah's town will
be scared of him," said Dad.

"Not if I hide him,"
said Iris.

She tried squeezing him
into her suitcase, but
he was too big.

She tried wrapping him up
like a present, but he was
too wriggly.

She even tried covering him
in decorations. But it was no good.

"Poor Lion," said Iris. "He'll be so lonely all on his own."

"Don't worry. He'll probably just sleep the whole time," said Dad.
"And you can bring your toy lion to keep you company," said Mom.

But Iris was still sad. She hated leaving her lion behind.

The lion didn't like to see Iris unhappy.
So, when the family set off to the train station, he followed them.

Nobody noticed him as he sneaked onto the train
and found a good place to hide among the luggage.

Iris was looking sadly out the window. The lion wanted to comfort her.

But before he
knew it, the train
had rocked him to sleep.

He was still fast asleep when the family reached their stop and got off the train. Auntie Sarah was there to meet them.
"Merry Christmas, Iris!" she said.

But Iris wasn't feeling very merry.
She kept thinking about her lion, at home all alone.

If only she knew!
The lion wasn't home at all.
He was still on the train and
heading far, far away
into the night.

When the lion woke up, he was very confused. The train had stopped, and everything was dark and quiet. Where had everyone gone?

He crept down from his hiding place and tiptoed outside.
He looked everywhere for Iris, but there was no one to be seen.

He had to find her—but which way should he go?

The lion looked back along the railway line. Perhaps if he followed the tracks, they would lead him to Iris.

The snow was
very deep, but he put
one cold paw in front of
the other until at last . . .

. . . he saw a village!

In the main square, he saw a huge tree festooned with colored lights, and people were singing all around it:

Fa-la-la-la-laaaa-la-la-la-laaa!

Perhaps Iris was singing with them?
The lion crept closer.

He found a hat and tried to blend in.
But when he joined the singing, what came out was a . . .

"ROAR!"

"A lion!" screamed the people,

and they chased after him, throwing snowballs. Luckily, lions can run fast.

They're good at hiding in trees, too.

As the crowd ran past, the lion noticed something in an upstairs window. It looked like Iris's toy lion! Perhaps this was Auntie Sarah's house? He had to be sure, but how could he check without waking everyone up?

Just then, the lion
saw a funny thing.
A man in a red coat
was climbing up and
down all the chimneys.

Maybe *that's* how the lion could get inside!

But before he could try,
there was a huge

WHOOSH!

and a

"HO-HO-HO!"

and the man in the red coat
swooped right over his head!

The lion slipped.
Then all the snow slid off the roof—

WHUMPF!

—and landed on top of him. He couldn't even move a whisker.

In the morning, Iris woke up
to find a new snowman in the garden.
"That's strange," she thought.

She went outside to have a better look.
It was a very odd snowman. It had a tail.

And when she patted the tail,
it waved at her!

As fast as she could, she dug at the
snow until she found . . .

. . . her lion!

"You're here!" said Iris.
"It's going to be the best
Christmas ever now!"

And it was—even if the lion did eat everyone's Christmas dinner.

"Never mind," said Iris.

"I prefer pizza anyway!"

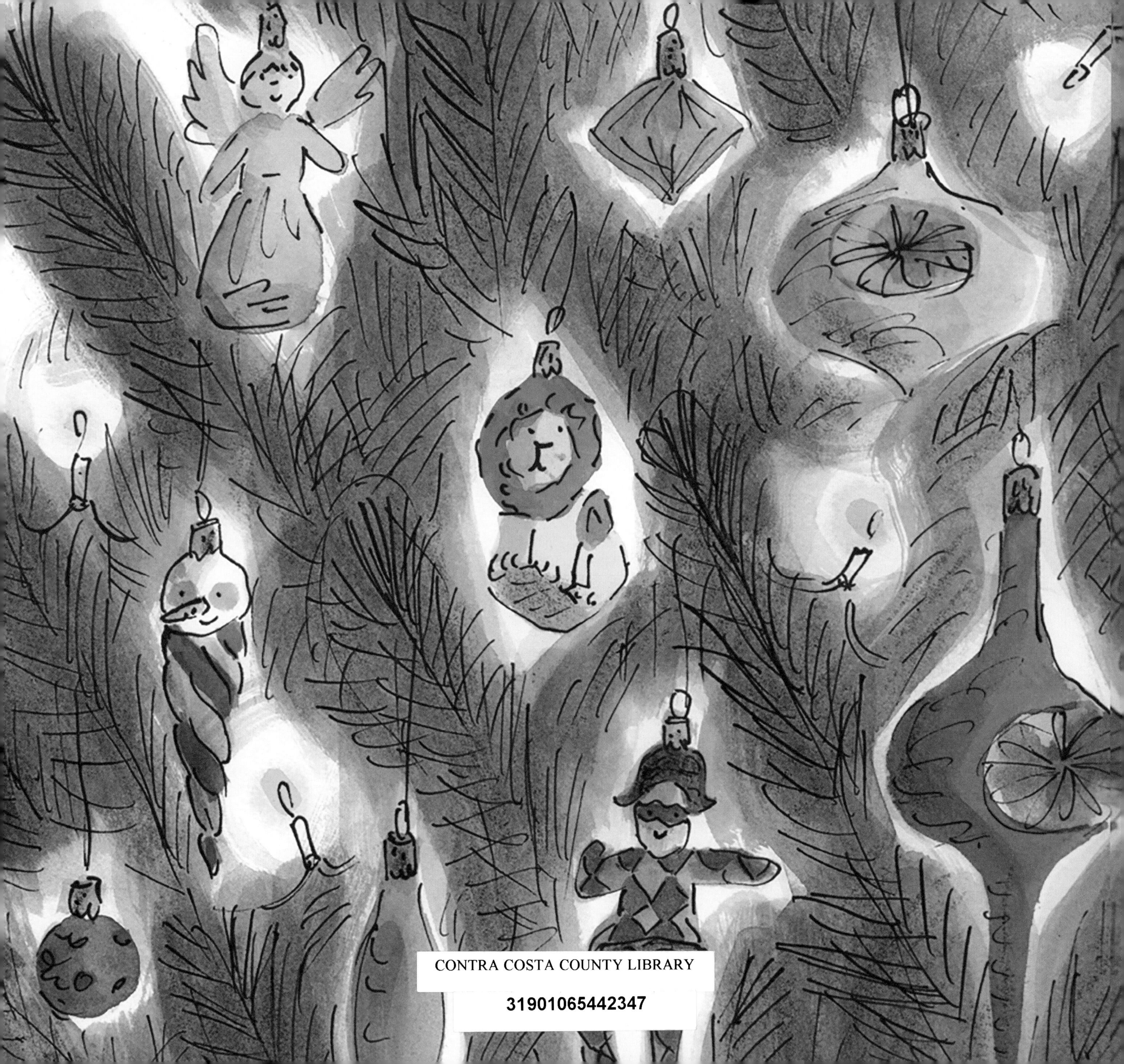